Bird Boy

Bird Boy

ELIZABETH STARR HILL

Pictures by LESLEY LIU

Farrar Straus Giroux   New York

3 5 7 9 11 10 8 6 4 2

Library of Congress Cataloging-in-Publication Data
Hill, Elizabeth Starr.
  Bird Boy / Elizabeth Starr Hill ; illustrated by Lesley Liu. —
1st ed.
     p.   cm.
  Summary: Chang, a mute Chinese boy whose father uses cormorants to
fish, is pleased when he is finally old enough to help with the Big Catch
and the raising of a new bird.
  ISBN 0-374-30723-7
  [1. Cormorants—Fiction. 2. Fishing—Fiction. 3. Mutism—
Fiction. 4. Physically handicapped—Fiction. 5. China—Fiction.]
I. Liu, Lesley, ill. II. Title.
PZ7.H55Bi   1999
[Fic]—dc21   98-51942

For Mei Mei Morris, with thanks —E.S.H.

For my father —L.L.

Bird Boy

1

Chang ate as fast as he could, his chopsticks almost flying between the bowl and his mouth. The cormorants squawked and called from their favorite perches on the houseboat. They were ready to go. Chang wanted to get started, too.

Chang had often fished with his father before, but tonight would be different. Once a year at this time, thousands of fish gathered in a wide place in the river. Nobody knew why. When it happened, all the cormorant fishermen went to that spot.

Sometimes the fish moved on before they

could be caught. But usually the men filled their baskets.

In other years, Chang's father had always told him, "You're not old enough to go with me. The Big Catch is hard work."

Tonight, finally, his father had agreed to take him along. But he warned Chang, "I'll be too busy to watch out for you. You must take care of yourself."

Chang nodded eagerly. Often in the past he had played with the birds on fishing trips, and gotten in his father's way. Tonight he made up his mind to do everything right. Then he might get a chance to help care for the next baby bird his father raised. That was an important job, even more important than the Big Catch. Chang had to prove he was ready for it.

Chang and his parents lived on a houseboat on the Li River, in southern China. The weather was very warm. The brazier his mother used for cooking made the inside of the boat even hotter. So the family sat on deck near the open stern, where they could enjoy a breeze from the river while they ate supper.

Chang finished his rice. His father sipped tea slowly.

From the path beside the river, a voice shouted, "Hai, Bird Boy!"

Chang saw Jinan, a farmer's son, spinning a hoop along the path.

Chang turned away. Jinan always made fun of him.

"What's the matter, Bird Boy, can't you talk?" Jinan jeered.

In fact, Chang could not talk, at least not to people. He had been born mute. He could make some sounds with his voice, but he could not form words. Only the birds seemed to understand his odd squawks and croaks.

Chang understood the birds, too. He had lived with them all his life. Their speech suited him.

Jinan knew this, of course. Many people in the village knew Chang as the boy who spoke only to birds.

"Can you spin a hoop, Bird Boy?" Jinan called. "If you come ashore, you can take a turn with mine."

Chang would have liked to try the hoop, but he didn't trust Jinan. The other boy always tricked him somehow. Besides, Chang was going fishing with his father, and that mattered more than anything.

He shook his head.

Jinan shrugged and said, "Some other time." He spun the hoop away on the path.

Chang's father was still sipping tea. It seemed that he would never finish. Chang wished he would hurry up so they could get started.

"Awk!" Kuo, the chief cormorant, squawked. "AWK! AWK!"

Chang repeated the bird's call, urging his father to hurry.

Chang's father laughed. "We'll leave when the sun reaches the top of the mountain," he promised.

Chang stepped to the side of the boat. He stood among the birds, watching the sun slide down the sky. Kuo hopped near him and brushed him with one wing.

Beyond the river there was a line of jagged

mountains. Soon the sun was like a fiery ball right on top of the highest peak. Chang pointed at it.

His father nodded. He took off his straw sandals and pulled on high black rubber boots. Chang was wearing boots already.

Then his father picked up a handful of long grass straws from a heap on the deck. He tied one around the neck of each bird.

The straws were not tight enough to harm the birds. They only kept them from swallowing big fish.

The cormorants were used to this. It was part of their job. When Chang called them in his strange voice, they stepped forward, one by one, to have the straws put on.

Later, when the catch was over, Chang and his father would untie the rings of grass. Then the birds would be free to go where they liked and fish for themselves.

Chang's father swung a pole across his shoulders. The cormorants, all eight of them, hopped onto it. Carrying them, Chang's father jumped onto his little fishing boat. It was a narrow raft made of five bamboo logs lashed together. The logs turned up slightly at the ends.

An oil lantern dangled from a thin rod on the prow of the boat.

The birds chose places. Kuo perched on the prow behind the lantern, his green eyes fixed on the water.

The boy sat beside the empty fish basket. Shen, one of the younger birds, poked at him, wanting to play.

Chang laughed and pulled at the bird's feathers. Shen jumped onto his shoulder and nibbled at his ear.

Chang forgot that he wasn't supposed to be playful tonight. He grabbed the bird. They tussled, banging against his father's leg.

"*Chang*," his father said in warning.

Chang sat up quickly. A minute later Shen poked at him again. This time Chang paid no attention.

His mother called, "Good luck!"

Chang's father untied the little raft from the houseboat. They were on their way!

2

Chang's father poled through the golden ripples toward the mountains, then around a long narrow bend. In rhythm to the poling, he sang a song about the river.

There had always been cormorant fishing in China. Chang's own family had lived and worked on the Li River for hundreds of years. Chang's father knew legends of great birds and mighty men, and fish as large as boats. All these were part of his song.

They glided through the dusk to where the water widened. Chang's father lighted the lantern. They heard other river songs and saw the lanterns of more and more fishermen. Chang hoped that someday he would know the ways of the river as well as they did and that he, too, would be a mighty man.

Suddenly Kuo gave a hoarse croak that meant he saw fish here. Other bird leaders in other boats croaked, too. The boats formed a circle. Their lights shone into the water.

Chang crouched beside Kuo and looked. The water was swarming with silver fish. Its surface was ruffled as though a giant wave were passing through it.

Chang's father shouted loudly and jumped up and down on the boat, telling the birds to dive. So did Chang. All the other fishermen cried out, too, chanting calls that their own birds understood.

Off went the birds, with noisy splashes! In a few seconds Kuo was up again. He had a big fish in his hooked bill.

"Ahh!" Chang's father exclaimed happily. He held out the end of the pole and scooped Kuo back into the boat. The bird was trained to give

up the fish, which was too large for him to swallow. Chang's father took it and threw it into the basket.

He gave Chang a covered box of cut-up fish. Chang fed Kuo a piece that he could swallow easily, as a reward. In an instant, the bird was off again.

Chang's father shouted and stamped louder than ever. The cries of the men and the birds made so much noise that echoes came back from the caves beside the river. It seemed to Chang that even the mountains were shouting.

Each cormorant returned with his catch to the fisherman he belonged to. Each was rewarded with a bit of fish.

As the Big Catch went on, Chang and his father had to work faster and faster. They seized fish from the birds, threw them into the basket, gave the birds their rewards, and cheered them on to dive some more.

Chang's hands got sore. His back hurt. But he never slowed down.

Finally, the fish grew scarce. Content with their full baskets, fishermen poled slowly away.

Chang's father clucked at his birds, telling them the fishing was over for tonight. He poled around the long bend of the river toward home.

"We have a fine catch to sell at the market tomorrow." He smiled. His teeth gleamed in the glow of the lantern. "You were a big help, Chang. I'm proud of you."

Chang was very tired and very happy. He stood tall beside his father.

The cormorants perched around him with their wings spread, drying their feathers. Soon the straws would be untied from their necks, and they could do as they pleased.

Chang looked at the moon in the sky, and the stars. He watched the lanterns, and the silver shine of the fish in the basket.

His father was proud of him.

The night seemed full of light.

3

The next day Chang woke up in a wonderful mood. He was almost sure now that his father would give him a chance to help raise the next baby bird. He would have to be careful, of course, not to get into trouble in the meantime.

After breakfast he went with his parents to the market. His father had the fish to sell, and his mother planned to buy vegetables. Kuo and Shen squawked to let Chang know they wanted to go, too, so he took them.

Croaking softly to the birds, he wandered around the market with Kuo on one shoulder and Shen on the other. He passed a stand where roast ducks were being sold.

He heard a voice call, "Hai, Bird Boy!"

It was Jinan, wheeling a shiny bicycle through the crowded market. Beside him was Mei Mei, his little sister. She looked pretty, with a wild-flower in her hair.

She smiled shyly at Chang. He smiled back.

"Are you selling those birds?" Jinan asked Chang.

Chang shook his head.

"That younger one would make a nice pet for Mei Mei," Jinan said with a scornful laugh. "Or maybe a nice stew for my mother to cook!" He reached out and tried to grab Shen.

"Don't!" Mei Mei said angrily to her brother.

Chang moved away quickly. With the birds still on his shoulders, he pushed through the crowds. He saw his mother near the vegetable stands. His father was nearby, too.

Chang had brought the birds here himself. He didn't want his parents to think he couldn't keep them safe.

He left the market and ran down a long hill to

the path beside the river. On his shoulders, Shen and Kuo grumbled at being jounced along so roughly. But Chang didn't dare stop.

He heard the bike behind him and looked back. Jinan was zooming down the hill, pedaling quickly toward him, waving his arms and showing off.

"I'll get you, Bird Boy!" Jinan shouted, laughing. "And I'll get one of those birds of yours, too!"

Chang thought Jinan would catch up to him for sure. Then suddenly Jinan lost control of the bike. It swerved wildly. He grabbed the handlebars and tried to turn onto the path, but he was riding too fast. The bike seemed to get away from him, and Jinan fell off.

The bike kept going. It just missed hitting Chang. It shot across the path and into the river.

"My bike!" Jinan yelled angrily. "My new bike!" He got up and ran to the edge of the river.

The water here was muddy and deep. There was no sign of the bike.

"You got in my way!" Jinan shouted at Chang.

Chang knew the accident wasn't his fault.

Still, he felt guilty and frightened. He started to run, with Kuo and Shen flapping on his shoulders.

Chang ran past a team of water buffalo. He passed a cartload of grunting pigs and a truck full of cabbages. Ducks scurried off the path as he raced by.

He looked back once and saw that Mei Mei had joined her brother at the river's edge. They were peering hopelessly at the water.

Chang was upset. He and the birds hurried on. At last they came to the hut where Bo Won the storyteller lived.

The old man was sitting in his open doorway, on the dirt floor. Bo Won was blind and lame. He could not fish or farm to make a living, so he told stories. People passing sometimes paused to listen. If they were in a good mood, they gave him a little money.

Chang had no money, but he threw himself breathlessly on the ground outside the doorway. Bo Won was kind. Chang felt safe here.

"Who's that?" Bo Won asked.

Chang said nothing, but Kuo and Shen

clucked and squawked. So Bo Won knew who it was.

"Ah, the Bird Boy," he said with a smile. "Well, I have a story for you."

Shen nestled against Chang's ear. Kuo hopped onto the ground and made himself comfortable. Chang stroked their glossy dark feathers. He told them that everything was all right now.

"Once there were three men who complained all the time," the storyteller began briskly. "They lived beside a forest. The men thought every forest creature had a better life than they did. The dragon of the forest heard their complaining, night and day. He got very tired of it. He decided to make them keep quiet."

Bo Won told how the dragon came out of the forest breathing fire. The men trembled with terror. Even so, they kept complaining.

During this part of the story, Chang saw Mei Mei walking toward them.

The birds stirred nervously. Chang felt nervous, too. He was afraid Jinan might appear next, ready to get revenge.

Mei Mei came over and sat beside Chang on

the ground. "Don't worry, Jinan's gone home," she whispered.

Chang nodded, relieved.

The storyteller told how the dragon changed the men into forest animals—first into deer, then rabbits, then mice. But the stupid three kept complaining.

Finally, the dragon changed them into stones. As far as anyone knew, they were still in the forest, but at least they couldn't complain anymore.

When the story ended, Mei Mei and Chang both giggled and clapped their hands. Mei Mei told the storyteller, "I have no money, but I can give you a flower."

"I like flowers," the storyteller said.

Mei Mei unpinned the blossom from her hair and put it in the old man's hand.

Together Mei Mei and Chang walked back along the path. Kuo and Shen followed them.

Chang and Mei Mei reached the place where the bike had disappeared.

Mei Mei said, "Jinan may try to dive for the bike later. He's not a very good swimmer, and the water's muddy. I don't think he'll ever find it." She added, "He loves that bike."

Chang had never had a bike, but he could imagine how awful it would be to lose one—and a new one, at that. He wasn't really sorry for Jinan. But he *was* afraid of him. He decided to try to get the bike out of the water.

He knew he would need a rope and a net to

pull out the bike. He touched Mei Mei's wrist and pointed to the ground.

Mei Mei sat down on the riverbank. "You want me to wait here?" she asked.

Chang nodded. He and the birds continued on the path, while Mei Mei stayed behind.

Soon Chang reached the wharf where his family's houseboat was moored. He leaped on board and picked up a net and a piece of rope. Sometimes his father used a net to catch small fish, but since he was at the market today he would not need this. Anyway, there were plenty of others on the boat.

Chang tied the rope to the net with a good strong fisherman's knot. Then he and the birds returned quickly to where Mei Mei was waiting.

Chang removed his shirt and kicked off his straw sandals. Wearing his loose blue trousers and holding the net and rope, he jumped into the river.

Kuo and Shen landed near him in the water.

Chang knew cormorants could dive as deep as eighty feet. They could see long distances underwater. Chang told them to look for something shiny on the bottom of the river.

The birds milled around in confusion. They knew this was not an ordinary fishing trip. Chang pointed down and made splashing motions.

Shen thought it was a game. He slapped the water with his wings and tried to play.

Chang pushed Shen away. He told Kuo to dive and search, dive and search.

At last Kuo shot toward the bottom, fast as black lightning. He stayed under for what seemed like a long time. Then he came up several feet away. He gave his squawk of triumph. It meant, "Here! Here you will find what you are looking for!"

Chang ducked under the surface, near Kuo. He stared down, but his eyes were not as sharp as the bird's. In the murky water, he couldn't tell if the bike was there or not.

He dropped the net, which was weighted to sink quickly to the bottom. When he pulled on the rope, he felt the net catch on something.

Holding the end of the rope, he swam to shore and climbed out.

Mei Mei grabbed on the rope and helped him pull. Together they hauled the heavy thing out of the water. But it was only a broken electric fan, shiny but useless.

Chang freed the net and swam out again. Again Kuo dove. Again the bird announced his find.

This time it was an old anchor, mostly rusted but with some metal shining through.

For the third time, Chang swam into the river and Kuo dove. Again the net caught on a large object.

Hardly daring to expect anything much, Chang and Mei Mei hauled the object up. As it came to the surface, there seemed to be shining circles in the murky water. The two friends looked at each other, suddenly excited.

"Those are wheels!" Mei Mei cried.

At last they had caught the bike!

Mei Mei thanked Chang. She thanked the birds, too. Then she wheeled the bike away to return it to Jinan.

Chang hoped Jinan would be satisfied now and would leave him alone.

The next day Jinan and Mei Mei came to the houseboat carrying kites.

Jinan called, "Thanks for getting the bike out."

Chang nodded. He was relieved by Jinan's friendly tone.

"There's a good breeze today," Jinan said. "Want to fly a kite with us, Bird Boy?"

Mei Mei added, "You can use my kite, if you don't have one."

Chang had a kite. His father had made it, and it was beautiful. It was shaped and painted to look like a golden fish.

He got the kite from the shelf where he kept it. He felt pleased and excited. It was rare for anyone to want to play with him.

With their kites, Chang and Jinan and Mei Mei climbed to the top of a hill. Here the wind blew fresh and strong. It lifted the kites into the blue sky.

"I wish I could fly," Mei Mei said, looking up.

"Can *you* fly, Bird Boy?" Jinan asked with a grin.

Chang nodded jokingly. Still holding the kite, he flapped his arms, as though he might take off at any moment.

Mei Mei and Jinan laughed.

On another morning, Jinan came alone and asked to borrow Chang's kite. He returned it with the string all knotted and tangled. "Guess I made a mess of this, Bird Boy." Jinan laughed.

Chang was used to untangling ropes and nets. He soon straightened out the string. But again he knew he couldn't trust Jinan.

5

Mei Mei stopped by with a few vegetables from her own garden patch. She called to Chang from the shore and held up the greens. "These are for you," she said shyly.

Chang beckoned her to come on board. The birds squawked and waddled forward to meet her.

Chang showed her around the houseboat. His mother and father made her welcome.

After that, she came often, usually with a handful of yard-long beans or some bok choy.

Once his mother made a delicious soup of the vegetables. She added dim sum, including the small dumplings Chang loved. She asked Mei Mei to stay for supper.

Mei Mei went to ask her mother. Chang was afraid she wouldn't come back. What fun could it be for her, a girl who talked, to be with someone who never said a word?

A sadness settled around his heart. He watched the path anxiously.

In half an hour, he saw her returning. She was carrying a covered dish. Chang crowed with happiness and waved both arms in greeting.

Chang had seen Mei Mei around the village all her life, but he had never really known her.

There were no other girls on the nearby farms. Probably boys didn't play with her much. Maybe she was lonely. Chang could understand that. Sometimes he was lonely, too.

She had brought a dish of spiced rice. Chang helped her onto the boat so it wouldn't spill.

Chang's mother sniffed at the rice. She said, "It smells delicious."

Chang's father exclaimed, "We'll have a feast tonight!"

There was a good sunset that evening. All its colors shone in the river. The birds sat on the side of the boat, black against the glowing sky. They croaked a little, but Chang didn't answer them. He kept very still until after supper.

Then he played his bamboo flute for Mei Mei. He tried to make a tune that would tell her she had friends here on the houseboat. With his music, he asked her to come again.

Chang and Mei Mei began to spend more time together. Sometimes they played checkers. When they had money, they walked to the market and bought almond cakes or a paper toy.

Sometimes they walked to Bo Won's house. He told them stories about a magic prince, and about a golden gong that made dreams come true. He said evil demons could fly only in a straight line, so a zigzag path was safest. He made them laugh.

Now and then, Jinan joined Chang and Mei

Mei for walks around the village. But Chang never felt comfortable with Jinan. He avoided going to Mei Mei's house because he didn't want to see her brother.

One day Chang saw his father take Kuo and a female bird to a little nesting boat that was tethered on the far shore. It was just like a fishing boat except that it was partially covered by a thatched-straw roof.

The boat belonged to Chang's father. There was no nest on it now, but Kuo and his mate would build one. Chang saw his father put a few small branches on the boat to give the birds the idea.

All that afternoon, Kuo gathered sticks and grasses and waterweeds from the river to make a strong nest. Chang was excited. He knew there would be eggs soon.

Chang's father raised a new bird every year. They were always hatched from eggs laid by mates of the fishing birds. A good bird is a fisherman's wealth, his father said.

Now Chang's father was busy mending a net. Chang went to him. He tugged at his sleeve and pointed at the nesting boat.

"I know," his father said. "When Kuo's mate has eggs, you want to help me raise the chick."

Chang nodded quickly.

"Will you be very careful?" his father asked.

Chang nodded again.

"Well, you did a good job on the Big Catch," his father said. "I'll be glad to have your help."

Chang skipped around the deck. He felt as bouncy as a bubble. The day was bright. A new bird would be born before long. And he was finally old enough to help with important things.

6

Cormorant eggs were almost always laid three to five days after the nesting couple settled down. So on the third day after Kuo and his mate built the nest, Chang woke up full of hope. Maybe there was an egg already!

At dawn his mother's rooster crowed. Next his mother's hens began clucking. Then the cormorants rustled and stirred.

Shen waddled in and tweaked at Chang's quilt. Chang romped with the bird until his mother called him for breakfast.

Right after they had eaten, Chang and his father went to the little boat to check the cormorants' nest. Neither parent bird was around. The nest was there, but it was empty.

"Not yet," his father said.

The same thing happened the next day.

"Not yet," his father said again.

On the fifth day, Chang was so excited he rose before the sun. He tiptoed to the rooster's perch and shook the bird awake. The bird blinked an eye at him and finally crowed.

Chang's parents woke. His mother fixed breakfast. When they had finished their tea and rice, his father said, "Well, Chang, this could be our lucky day."

Again he and Chang poled toward the nesting boat. Kuo's mate was still sitting on the nest, so they waited quietly until she flew off to feed in the river. Then Chang's father pushed their boat close to the nest.

Chang held his breath as he looked in it. Delight shot through him. Eggs! There were four chalky-blue eggs!

Chang's father lifted one and looked at it closely. He put it back. He did the same with another, and a third, and the fourth.

Finally he chose. "This one will be good," he said. From his pocket he took a large wad of cotton and wrapped the egg in it.

Every bird they owned had been born on their houseboat, so Chang knew they would take the egg away from the nest. A fishing bird has to be with its human family from the beginning. Then it can learn by watching the adult fishing birds. The remaining eggs would be left for the female bird to raise.

Chang's father told him, "You're my helper, Chang. You can carry this." And he handed him the cotton-wadded egg.

Chang had never been allowed to touch one of the special eggs before. He took it very, very carefully. He lowered himself to the bottom of the little fishing boat. He sat still, hardly daring to breathe, holding the egg in both hands.

His father poled back to the houseboat. In a sheltered spot on deck, one of the laying hens had a nest. Chang's father scattered some chicken feed near it. When the hen hopped out to get the feed, Chang slipped the cormorant egg into her nest.

The hen didn't notice. She went on pecking at the feed.

Chang watched the hen anxiously. What if she never got on the nest again?

But at last she did, her soft feathers fluffing around the cormorant egg as well as her own eggs. For about four weeks, the hen would keep the egg warm while the cormorant chick grew inside it.

Chang ran and got his mother. He took her to see the egg.

"Wonderful!" she said. They joined hands and danced. Several cormorants danced with them, getting under their feet. Chang and his mother stumbled and fell in a heap, laughing.

Every morning Chang fed the hen. While she pecked at the food, he looked in the nest. He thought he never had seen a more perfect egg.

He brought Mei Mei to see it. His mother explained to Mei Mei that this was the start of a great fishing bird, like Kuo and the others.

Mei Mei looked at the egg, with wide dark eyes. "When will it be born?" she asked.

"In about a month," Chang's mother said.

Mei Mei asked Chang, "When it's big enough, can I carry it on my shoulder sometimes? When I'm with you, of course."

Chang nodded and smiled.

After four weeks had passed, Chang's father told him, "We have to move the egg now. It's about ready to hatch."

Chang knew that if a cormorant was born in a hen's nest, she might realize it was not her own chick and kill it.

They lined a shallow bamboo basket with cotton. Then Chang set the egg in the basket. He followed his father to a cabin that could be closed off from the rest of the houseboat.

His father lighted a lantern in the dim space. Chang put the basket under it.

His father said, "When the bird is born, we'll need small fish to feed it."

Chang covered the egg with more cotton. He rushed to get a fine mesh net and a handful of crumbs. He threw the crumbs over the side of the boat.

Minnows rose in the water like specks of silver. Chang tossed the net over them. Most of them got away. But Chang pulled some up and dumped them in a can filled with water. He threw more crumbs and tossed the net again.

Then he raced to the cabin, where his father was sitting by the cotton-lined basket.

His father said, "The egg hasn't hatched yet."

Chang wandered off and sat on deck.

It seemed like a long wait. But at last his father called, "Chang! Come and see!"

Chang almost flew across the deck. He flung open the wooden door and looked in the basket.

Lantern light flickered over it. Chang saw the pieces of broken shell—and a newborn baby bird! It was scrawny and bare, with no feathers. It wiggled its wings and feet and head. Its eyes were closed, but its beak was open.

Gently Chang touched one tiny wing. The bird made a funny squawking sound.

Chang made the same sound. So he and the chick said hello to each other.

7

Chang knew that baby cormorants often died in the first week of life. They must be kept warm and quiet, and fed often.

"Any shock can kill the young bird," Chang's father said. "Don't pick it up or let the other birds near it."

Chang's parents took turns caring for the nestling at night. Chang helped during the day. He did just as his father told him.

Each morning he saw changes in the little bird. Soon it grew dark downy feathers. Its eyes opened. The eyes would turn bright green or blue when the cormorant was older, but now they looked like shiny black buttons.

Chang liked watching the chick. It was always moving. It seemed to want to walk and fly. Maybe—who knew?—it even had some idea of catching fish. Of course, it was much too young to do any of those things, but it kept trying.

"This little bird never gives up." Chang's father chuckled. "It will be getting around in no time."

Mei Mei was thrilled by the chick's birth. She came to the houseboat almost every morning. Sometimes Jinan came, too, although Chang didn't really want him to. He was always glad when Jinan went away.

Mei Mei sat very still while Chang fed the bird. He let her feed it, too. Sometimes, when the chick looked sleepy after a meal, she hummed a gentle lullaby. Then she and Chang watched together as the bird fell asleep.

Before long, the chick seemed to know Mei

Mei. It cheeped and stretched up its open beak toward her. It waggled its wings.

One day Jinan arrived alone, on his bike. He called from the shore, "Want to take a ride, Chang? You can use my bike if you like!"

Chang's parents were out in the fishing boat with the older cormorants. His mother had told him to watch the baby bird while they were gone and to be sure to feed it on time.

It wasn't time to feed the chick yet, and Chang longed to ride the bike. He'd ridden bikes before, but not often. He jumped off the boat eagerly.

Jinan pushed the bike toward him and said, "I'll wait right here. Enjoy yourself."

Chang got on the bike and rode along the path. He was wobbly at first. But soon he got better.

"You're doing fine!" Jinan called helpfully. "Just keep going!"

Chang found a good pedaling rhythm, and the bike straightened out. He rode faster. The wind sang in his ears.

He passed green rice paddies and fields of soybeans, and a stand of twisted pines. As he whizzed along, Chang felt as if he owned the world.

Then a vague worry came over him. The fun of riding began to dim. He thought of the baby bird, helpless and alone. He remembered bad things Jinan had done in the past.

Dread grew inside him.

Chang turned and rode back to the wharf as fast as he could go. Jinan was sitting on the wharf. He stood up with a cheerful smile as Chang appeared.

"Did you have a good ride?" he asked.

Chang nodded and gave him the bike.

Jinan took it and rode off, whistling. Then Chang noticed a bulge in Jinan's pocket. Above the pocket, a tiny head was bobbing.

Horrified, Chang made a shrieking sound. But Jinan kept going.

Chang leaped on board the houseboat and rushed to the baby bird's basket. It was empty. Chang knew that the bird was in Jinan's pocket.

Trembling and cold with fear, Chang went

to Jinan's house. The bike was by the back door.

Chang pounded on the door.

Mei Mei opened it.

"Chang!" she said in surprise. She started to smile, then saw how upset Chang was. "What's wrong?" she asked.

But of course he couldn't explain it to her. He made a wide hopeless gesture.

"Is it Jinan?" Mei Mei asked.

Chang nodded and spread his hands in despair.

"He's had an accident?" Mei Mei cried.

Chang shook his head.

"He's done something bad, then," Mei Mei whispered.

Chang nodded and pulled at Mei Mei's hand, trying to make her understand he wanted to look for Jinan.

"We'll try his room," Mei Mei said quickly.

As they walked through the house, Mei Mei called, "Jinan! Jinan!"

There was no answer. And Jinan was not in his room.

"Let's look in the barn," Mei Mei suggested.

They searched the barn. No one was there either.

Then Mei Mei said, "Jinan has a special hiding place. When he's really in trouble, he goes there."

She led Chang through a vegetable garden to a rickety shed. She pushed open the door.

Jinan was sitting inside the shed, in the dimness. The baby cormorant lay in front of him on the ground, limp and still.

8

For a terrible moment, Chang thought the bird was dead. Then he saw a slight movement of the small chest. The bird was breathing, but just barely.

Jinan looked pale and scared. "I didn't mean to hurt the chick," he mumbled. "I would have brought it back. I only meant to give you a scare, Chang. It was just a joke."

"A *joke?*" Mei Mei said furiously. "The bird may die!"

"I didn't mean it," Jinan mumbled again.

Chang picked up the little bird and cradled it in his hands.

Mei Mei cried, "Oh, Chang—Chang—can I help?"

Chang shook his head. His heart thumped sickeningly as he walked alone to the houseboat.

Chang put the bird in the basket and tucked cotton around it. But still the chick lay as though dead. It seemed to Chang that its breathing was growing fainter.

Thoughts poured into Chang's mind. He imagined all the happy days he had expected to spend with the young bird.

He began to talk, in a murmur of sounds that only a cormorant would understand. He begged the bird to wake up, to live. He promised to take it out in the fishing boat with the older birds. He described the swarms of silver fish they would catch.

The chick stirred, pushing its way out of stillness. Its eyes opened.

Chang told the bird that they would swim and play together. They would be best friends.

Slowly the little cormorant struggled up from its nest of cotton. It gave a faint croak.

Chang spoke louder and faster. He told about the good smell of food cooking in his mother's wok. He said that when the chick was bigger, it could share a piece of dim sum with Shen, who was always stealing from the family's bowls.

Chang heard Mei Mei's voice calling from shore. "Chang, how is the bird?" she asked in a scared tone.

Chang ran out on deck. He beckoned to her urgently.

Mei Mei came aboard and sat quietly near the basket. Chang sat beside her. He told the chick that it could ride on Mei Mei's shoulder some-day. They would have a party on the houseboat, and everyone would dance.

Slowly the bird stood up. In a rush of joy, Chang held out a piece of fish. The cormorant stretched its beak wide and gulped it down.

Chang made up more adventures. He talked and talked.

At last the cormorant grew sleepy, and Mei Mei had to go.

When she had left, Chang told the chick to rest for a while.

He walked out on the deck. The air was fresh and damp. Mist hung on the river and around the mountains. He looked at the bamboo groves and rice paddies, the fishing boats and birds. His world.

Chang wished he could touch everything, hold everything. The day was so beautiful, and he was so happy.

Then Jinan appeared.

"I hear your problem came out all right," he called cheerfully from the shore. "That's good."

Chang stared at Jinan. He did not smile.

"Can I come aboard?" Jinan asked. "I brought some cards, if you want to play."

Chang posted himself on deck near the edge of the wharf. There was no way Jinan could get past him onto the boat.

Jinan raised his eyebrows. He grinned uncertainly. "You're not going to hold that joke of mine against me, are you?" he asked. "Don't be that way, Bird Boy."

Chang had often been afraid of Jinan, but he

wasn't afraid now. He felt as strong as the Great Wall of China. He didn't move.

"I'm *sorry*," Jinan said at last, in a whining tone. "What more do you want?"

Chang stood motionless, arms folded, head high.

Jinan shifted from one foot to the other. His boldness faded. Finally, he blustered, "I probably would have won the card game anyway." He shuffled off, kicking stones.

The small bird grew healthy and strong. When it was old enough, Chang took it out on deck to meet the other cormorants.

Kuo came forward to see the new arrival. The big bird and the little bird strode toward each other. They faced each other, eye to eye.

They didn't seem much alike now. But Chang thought the chick might become a leader someday, like Kuo.

The little bird had spirit. It would try hard. And Chang had found that trying made all the difference.

FIC   Hill, Elizabeth
HIL   Starr.

           Bird Boy.

                    34000005024260
                     10/27/2000

DATE			

12/00